My "u" Sound Box®

WRITTEN BY JANE BELK MONCURE • ILLUSTRATED BY REBECCA THORNBURGH

The Child's World®
childsworld.com

Published by The Child's World®
1980 Lookout Drive • Mankato, MN 56003-1705
800-599-READ • www.childsworld.com

ISBN HARDCOVER: 9781503823242
ISBN PAPERBACK: 9781503831469
LCCN: 2017960386

Printed in the United States of America
PA02371

A NOTE TO PARENTS AND EDUCATORS:

Magic moon machines and five fat frogs are just a few of
the fun things you can share with children by reading books
with them. Reading aloud helps children in so many ways!
It introduces them to new words, motivates them to develop
their own reading skills, and expands their attention span
and listening abilities. So it's important to find time each day
to share a book or two . . . or three!

As you read with young children, you can help develop
their understanding of how print works by talking about the
parts of the book—the cover, the title, the illustrations, and the
words that tell the story. As you read, use your finger to point
to each word, modeling a gentle sweep from left to right.

Simple word games help develop important prereading
skills, including an understanding of rhyme and alliteration
(when words share the same beginning sound, such as "six"
and "sand"). Try playing with words from a book you've
just shared: "What other words start with the same sound
as moon?" "Cat and hat, do those words rhyme?" The
possibilities are endless—and so are the rewards!

My "u" Sound Box®

This book concentrates on the short "u" sound in the story line. Words beginning with the long "u" sound are included at the end of the book.

Little had a box. "I will find things

that begin with my **u** sound," she said.

"I will put them into my sound box."

"First, I will find an umbrella."

"I will run, run, run to find an umbrella."

Why did Little   get under the box?

Why was the box upside down?

Little  found an umbrella.

She found lots of umbrellas.

She put one umbrella over her head. Did she put the other umbrellas into her box? She did.

Just then, the sun came out.

Little  put the umbrella down.

But then the rain came down again.

Little  put the umbrella up.

Then she saw some underclothes.

They were getting wet.

She took the underclothes off the
line. She put them into her box.

Little  took the underclothes upstairs.

She put the underclothes away.

"Now," she said, "I can play under my umbrella." She went out in the rain.

"I can run through a puddle," she said. "What fun!"

Then she found an ugly duckling.

The ugly duckling was grumpy.

She put the ugly duckling into her box.

"Do not be grumpy," she said.

"You will grow up to be beautiful."

Just then, her uncle came by.

He was getting wet, so Little  gave her  uncle an umbrella.

Then an umpire came by.
"Can you help us?" he said.

"We are playing baseball in the rain. We need umbrellas."

Little  said, "I have a box full of umbrellas."

She gave the  umpire an umbrella.

Then she gave everyone an umbrella.

What fun they had
in the rain!

Little U's Word List

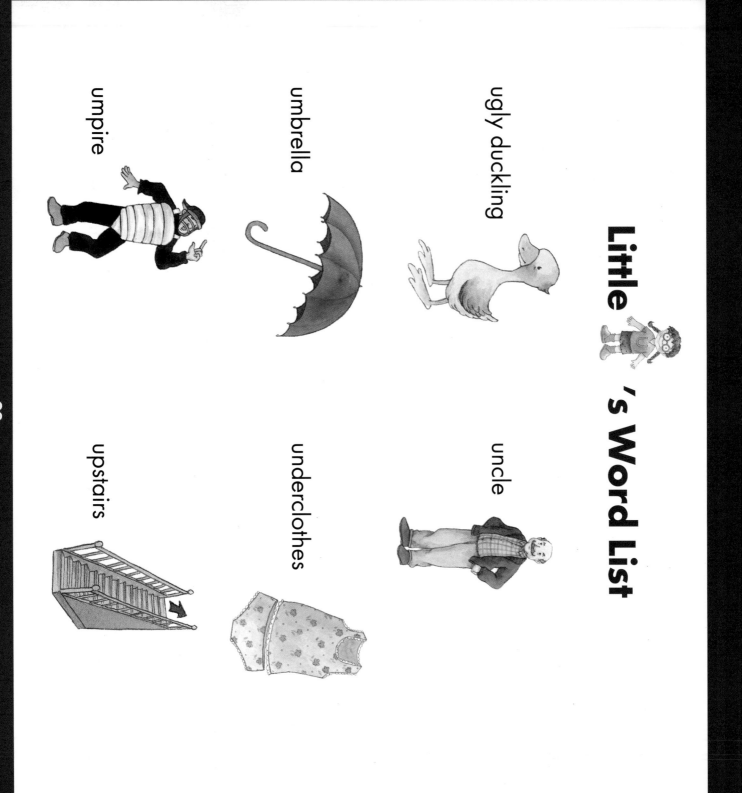

ugly duckling

umbrella

umpire

uncle

underclothes

upstairs

Other Words with the Short U Sound

udder

undershirt

urn

Uncle Sam

uphill

usher

Words with the Long U Sound

Little u has another sound in some words. She says her name, "u."
Can you read these words? Listen for Little u's name.

ukulele

unicycle

United States

unicorn

uniform

universe

More to Do!

Little ___'s umbrellas kept everyone dry in the rain. You can make a toy umbrella with a little help from an adult.

What you need:
- a paper plate
- a drinking straw
- tape
- a pencil
- markers
- scissors

Directions:

1. Ask an adult to help you use the pencil to divide the paper plate into six triangle-shaped sections (like the slices of a pizza).

2. Use your markers to make each section a bright color.

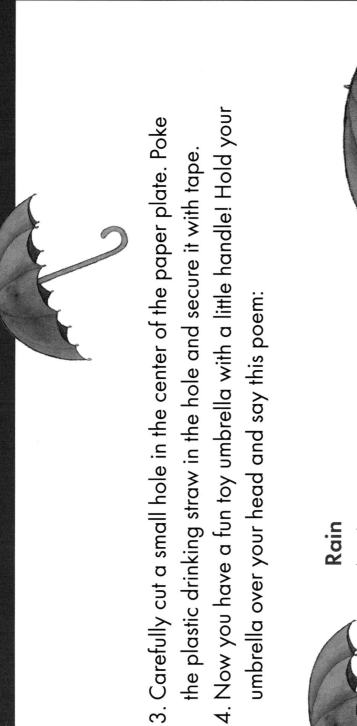

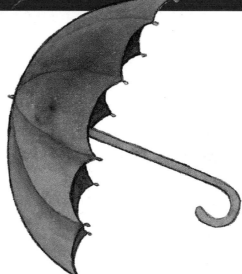

3. Carefully cut a small hole in the center of the paper plate. Poke the plastic drinking straw in the hole and secure it with tape.

4. Now you have a fun toy umbrella with a little handle! Hold your umbrella over your head and say this poem:

Rain

by Robert Louis Stevenson

The rain is falling all around
It falls on the field and tree,
It rains on the umbrellas here,
And on the ships at sea.

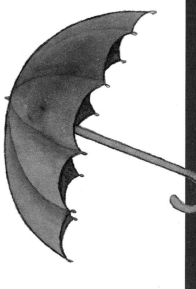

About the Author

Best-selling author Jane Belk Moncure (1926–2013) wrote more than 300 books throughout her teaching and writing career. After earning a master's degree in early childhood education from Columbia University, she became one of the pioneers in that field. In 1956, she helped form the Virginia Association for Early Childhood Education, which established the first statewide standards for teachers of young children.

Inspired by her work in the classroom, Mrs. Moncure's books became standards in primary education, and her name was recognized across the country. Her success was reflected not only in her books' popularity with parents, children, and educators, but also by numerous awards, including the 1984 C. S. Lewis Gold Medal Award.

About the Illustrator

Rebecca Thornburgh lives in a pleasantly spooky old house in Philadelphia. If she's not at her drawing table, she's reading—or singing with her band, called Reckless Amateurs. Rebecca has one husband, two daughters, and two silly dogs.